Jolly Old Santa Claus

This book belongs to

_____

Jolly Old Santa Claus

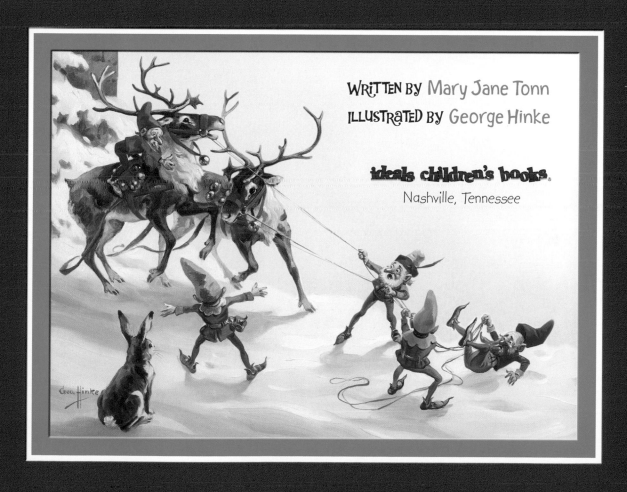

WRITTEN BY Mary Jane Tonn

ILLUSTRATED BY George Hinke

ideals children's books.
Nashville, Tennessee

ISBN 0-8249-5513-7

Published by Ideals Children's Books
An imprint of Ideals Publications
A division of Guideposts
535 Metroplex Drive, Suite 250
Nashville, Tennessee 37211
www.idealsbooks.com

Copyright © 2005 by Ideals Publications

Color separations by Precision Color
Graphics, Franklin, Wisconsin

Printed and bound in Italy by LEGO

Library of Congress CIP data on file

Designed by Georgina Chidlow-Rucker

10 9 8 7 6 5 4 3 2 1

"Ho, ho, ho!" chuckled Jolly Old Santa Claus as he stroked his long white beard and laughed.

Mrs. Santa Claus and all the brownies came over to see what Santa was laughing about. "What is so funny?" they asked.

"This is a letter from a little boy," said Jolly Old Santa Claus. "Can you guess what he wants to know?"

The brownies all tried to guess. "Will he get a train for Christmas? Will we find his new house?"

"No," chuckled Jolly Old Santa Claus. "This little boy wants to know if we are busy at the North Pole!"

"Are we busy!" shouted all the little brownies. "We most certainly are!"

The North Pole is the busiest place in the world, just before Christmas. Come with me, and we'll visit the North Pole.

THEN YOU CAN SEE FOR YOURSELF WHAT IS HAPPENING THERE.

Let's stop at the cookie kitchen. Look at the brownies scurrying about with smudges of flour on their aprons and sugar on their hands. How hard they are working!

Oops, Old Grampa Brownie fell. The big sack of flour is heavy, and he was walking backwards into the kitchen.

There's Jingles sitting on top of the oven and telling the brownies just how to place the trays of cookies so they won't burn.

Aren't you glad when Christmastime comes and you can eat cookies?

But we must hurry on.

THERE IS MUCH TO SEE.

Here is the candy kitchen! Santa and the brownies are making candy canes and lollipops, peppermint drops, and cotton candy. Look at the brownies pouring milk into the pot for fudge. Uh oh, one little brownie has tripped over Lady Whiskers and spilled the frosted brownies.

Santa and the brownies are making a lot of candy to fill the stockings of good little boys and girls.

NOW LET'S GO TO THE TOY SHOP WHERE WONDERFUL TOYS ARE MADE.

Isn't this a wonderful place? Every brownie is busy, except for Lazy Brownie. He's riding the rock-a-bye pony when he should be working.

Jolly Old Santa Claus is checking his list of toys: airplanes, trains, drums, building blocks, dolls, teddy bears, and rubber bouncing balls.

There are so many toys to finish before Christmas. Can you see Lady Whiskers? She is Santa's favorite cat. Do you see Merry One falling down the stairs? I think old Jack-in-the-box frightened him.

Look at the clock on the wall. Chief Brownie has seen it, and he is telling the other brownies to hurry. It's getting late, and Christmas will soon be here.

While the brownies in the toy shop finish painting and fixing the toys, let's see what they are doing in the Christmas tree room.

Isn't this a beautiful room! There are so many bright colors and pretty ornaments for the Christmas trees. Look, back there in the corner, the brownies are blowing the glass ornaments.

This is a special job, and only the most careful brownies can work here. The glass ornaments must be handled very carefully or they will break.

Can you see Lady Whiskers? She's high in the rafters watching. If she walked on the floor, her long tail would break the ornaments. Chief Brownie wouldn't like that at all.

There's Lazy Brownie. He's sitting on top of the tool shelf so no one can see him.

LET'S GO VISIT THE OTHER PLACES AT THE NORTH POLE.

Here is the office of Jolly Old Santa Claus. He is reading letters from boys and girls.

Mrs. Santa Claus marks down the names and addresses of all little boys and girls who have moved to new houses since last year, so Santa Claus will be sure to find them.

Do you see Lady Whiskers? She is sitting on top of Santa's chair, and Lazy Brownie is hiding under Santa's desk.

Do you see Jingles handing letters to Impy Brownie to give to Santa to read? And there's Chief Brownie tugging in a heavy sack of letters for Santa.

Santa looks happy. He must be reading a letter from a very good little boy or girl. Do you think it is your letter?

Santa Claus has just asked Chief Brownie if the Christmas trees are all ready to be packed. Let's scurry along and see.

Christmas trees grow all over the forest.

Look at the little animals in the forest. They love to watch the brownies collecting the trees.

Do you see Old Grampa Brownie slip in the deep snow? Look, he's lost his cap! He's the funniest brownie, isn't he? And he never remembers to wear his glasses.

I wonder where Lazy Brownie is. He's probably not working at all, but talking to the reindeer. Can you find him?

While the brownies finish loading the trees, let's go see what Mrs. Santa Claus is doing.

Here is Mrs. Claus in front of Santa's castle. She is making sure that everything will be ready for Santa to leave on time. He must not be late!

The brownies are putting the toys into the sleigh. Look at that teddy bear. He's so big that two brownies have to carry him to the sleigh.

Chief Brownie has Santa's Route in his hand and will know just where the reindeer must stop.

Jingles is leading the reindeer out to hook them up to the sleigh.

What is Mrs. Santa Claus holding in her hands? Are those earmuffs and a heavy scarf to keep Santa Claus warm on his long trip tonight?

For tonight is the night. At long last it is here. It is the night before Christmas.

The stars are twinkling in the sky. All the world is hushed and still, waiting for this magical night.

For tonight, yes, tonight he comes. Swiftly through the skies they will fly— Jolly Old Santa Claus and his eight reindeer.

And more quietly than softly falling snow, he will land atop your house.

AND THEN, SILENTLY, oh, SO SILENTLY, hE WiLL PUT a PaCK OF TOYS ON his BACK AND SLiDE DOWN YOUR ChiMNEY.

Santa will fill your stocking with goodies and place wonderful surprises beneath your tree.

Then, just as quietly and just as quickly as he came, in the wink of an eye, he will be gone.

All through the night he flies, bringing happiness and joy and love into the homes of all little children.

Long before the sun rises in the Christmas morning sky, Jolly Old Santa Claus will have visited the homes of every good little boy and girl all over the world. Then he will fly back to his home at the North Pole.

There will be such excitement when he comes home! The little brownies will want to know all about Jolly Old Santa Claus's trip.

"Did it snow, Santa?"

"Was it very cold?"

"Were the little boys and girls asleep in their beds?"

"Were the children happy with their toys?"

Look at Lady Whiskers! She has a surprise for Santa. She's brought him four soft, cuddly little kittens.

While the brownies feed the reindeer and settle them down for sleep, Jolly Old Santa Claus will tell them all about his trip.

Now they are all busy brownies, even Lazy Brownie who is shining Santa's boots and polishing the bells from his sleigh.

Chief Brownie is telling his helpers to unpack the unused toys very carefully so they can be used next year.

Look at Impy Brownie. He's spilling the bucket of red paint! He's so excited to have Santa back from his trip.

Santa is very tired and very hungry after his long night's journey.

MRS. SANTA CLAUS has MADE hoT choCOLATE AND COOKiES FOR hiM!

Soon all of the work will be finished. Then Jolly Old Santa Claus and Mrs. Santa Claus will rest for awhile. As the sun comes over the North Pole, Jolly Old Santa Claus, Mrs. Claus, and all of the Brownies will say "Merry Christmas" to one another.

Early Christmas Morning, Mrs. Claus will sit down at the organ while the brownies pump the foot pedal. Music fills the air, and Jolly Old Santa Claus will sing out:

SILENT NIGHT, HOLY NIGHT,

ALL IS CALM, ALL IS BRIGHT

ROUND YON VIRGIN, MOTHER AND CHILD,

HOLY INFANT SO TENDER AND MILD.

SLEEP IN HEAVENLY PEACE.

SLEEP IN HEAVENLY PEACE.

THEN JOLLY OLD SANTA CLAUS CALLS OUT, "MERRY CHRISTMAS TO ALL BOYS AND GIRLS AROUND THE WORLD."